# My Friend, LOONIE

Nina LaCour

illustrated by

Ashling Lindsay

WALKER BOOKS

AND SUBSIDIARIES

LONDON • BOSTON • SYDNEY • AUCKLAND

It began on the day her parents came home with a surprise.

A balloon that floated up and up
all the way to the ceiling.

"Hello, Loonie,"
the little girl said.
"Welcome to your home."

Together, they watched out
the window as a squirrel nibbled
an acorn and a family of finches
pecked for seeds on the grass.

With Loonie's string around the girl's wrist,
they bobbed out the door for a walk.
"What a nice balloon!" said their neighbour.
"This is Loonie!" said the girl.

She set a place for Loonie
at the dinner table

and made sure Loonie saw all the pages
of their bedtime story.

At lights-out, the girl tucked Loonie in,
but Loonie wanted to stay up.
"Well, OK," whispered the girl.
"As long as you're very quiet...

Good night, Loonie."

Before school, she kissed Loonie goodbye.
"Remember to watch Loonie!" she told the dog.

*Woof!*

After school, Loonie kept the
girl company as she ate her
snack and did her homework.

When the girl's favourite song
came on, they danced together.

"Nice moves, Loonie...

What should we do next?"
asked the girl.

"Oh, you want to see my garden?"
Loonie bobbed.
"Sure, let's go!"

"LOONIE!"

The little girl watched
as Loonie grew smaller

and smaller

and smaller
in the sky.

Her parents held her close.

"I miss Loonie," the girl said.
"We know," they told her.
"Come garden with us."

Together they pressed flower seeds into the soft dirt.
And the girl was sad for a long time.

From her spot at the window,
the mornings were quiet and grey.

Neighbourhood walks felt lonely.

Until, one day, out in the garden …
the little girl noticed something.
A green stem and green leaves,
topped with the most beautiful blossom,
the very same colour as Loonie.

"Come and see!" she called out.

Her parents smiled. The little girl smiled, too.
"Loonie was a good friend," the girl said.
And her parents bobbed their heads,
just like Loonie used to do.

The next morning, she woke up
with a glow in her heart.

As she danced to her favourite song,
she thought of Loonie's moves,
and the remembering
made her own jumps bouncier.

She checked the window for birds
and squirrels and saw yellow in
places she'd never noticed before.

And when it was time for
their walk, she stepped off
the porch and discovered ...
that the whole world was brighter.

For H.S. who made the world brighter
N.L.
For my sister Niamh
A.L.

Balloons have signified celebration for at least one hundred years.

Because a deflated balloon can be a choking hazard for very young children,
it is recommended that children younger than eight years old do not play
with deflated or uninflated balloons unsupervised.

Additionally, please protect wildlife and marine environments by
disposing of used balloons in your household waste.

First published 2023 by Walker Books Ltd
87 Vauxhall Walk, London SE11 5HJ

2 4 6 8 10 9 7 5 3 1

Text © 2023 Nina LaCour
Illustrations © 2023 Ashling Lindsay

The right of Nina LaCour and Ashling Lindsay to be identified as author and illustrator of this work has been
asserted in accordance with the Copyright, Designs and Patents Act 1988

This book has been typeset in Arvo

Printed in China

British Library Cataloguing in Publication Data:
a catalogue record for this book is available from the British Library

ISBN 978-1-5295-1367-7

www.walker.co.uk